A Note to Parents and Teachers

The *Dorling Kindersley Readers* series is a reading programme for children, which is highly respected by teachers and educators around the world. The LEGO Company has a global reputation for offering high quality, innovative products, designed to stimulate a child's creativity and development through play.

Now Dorling Kindersley has joined forces with The LEGO Company, to produce the first-ever graded reading scheme to be based around LEGO play themes. Each *Dorling Kindersley Reader* is guaranteed to capture a child's imagination, while developing his or her reading skills, general knowledge and love of reading.

The books are written and designed in conjunction with literacy experts, including Cliff Moon M.Ed., Honorary Fellow of the University of Reading.

Cliff Moon spent many years as a teacher and teacher educator, specializing in reading. He has written more than 140 books for children and teachers, and he reviews regularly for teachers' journals.

The four levels of *Dorling Kindersley Readers* are aimed at different reading abilities, enabling you to choose the books that are right for each child.

Level 1 – Beginning to Read
Level 2 – Beginning to Read Alone
Level 3 – Reading Alone
Level 4 – Proficient Readers

The "normal" age at which a child begins to read can be anywhere from three to eight years old, so these levels are only guidelines.

Dorling Kindersley

LONDON, NEW YORK, SYDNEY, DELHI, PARIS,
MUNICH and JOHANNESBURG

Senior Editor Cynthia O'Neill
Senior Art Editor Nick Avery
Senior Managing Editor
Karen Dolan
Managing Art Editor
Cathy Tincknell
DTP Designer Jill Bunyan
Production Chris Avgherinos
Picture Researcher Andrea Sadler

Reading Consultant
Cliff Moon M.Ed.

First published in Great Britain in 2000 by
Dorling Kindersley Limited
9 Henrietta Street
London WC2E 8PS

2 4 6 8 10 9 7 5 3 1

© 2000 The LEGO Company
® LEGO is a registered trademark belonging to The LEGO Company
and used here by special permission..

www.lego.com

A CIP catalogue record for this book is
available from the British Library.

ISBN 0-7513-7254-4

Colour reproduction by Dot Gradations, UK
Printed and bound by L Rex, China

The publisher would like to thank the following for their kind
permission to reproduce their photographs:
c=centre; b=bottom; l=left; r=right; t=top

E.T. Archive: 25br;
Mary Evans Picture Library: 11tr, 12br;
Robert Harding Picture Library: Roy Rainford 7br, 32crb.

For our complete
catalogue visit
www.dk.com

DK **DORLING KINDERSLEY** *READERS* **LEGO**

CASTLE
UNDER
ATTACK

Written by Nicola Baxter • Illustrated by Roger Harris

BEGINNING 2 TO READ ALONE

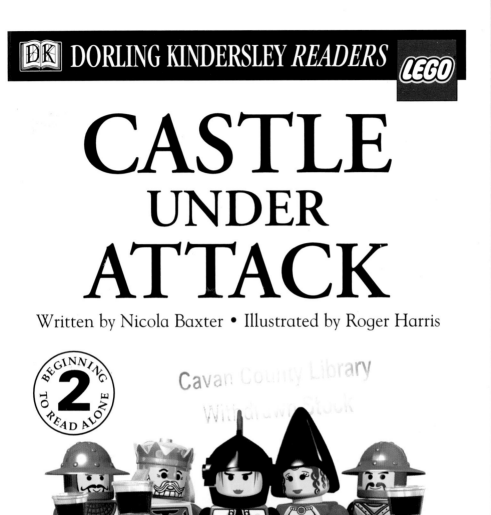

A Dorling Kindersley Book

In a faraway land,
in the middle of a dark forest,
there was a mighty castle.

King Leo and Queen Leonora
lived in the castle,
with their daughter, Princess Storm.

One day, the king decided
to hold a feast at the castle.
There would be a tournament,
where knights could show their skill.

"It will be a wonderful day,"
King Leo told Queen Leonora.
"Only one thing can go wrong."
"I know," said the queen.
"Maybe Cedric the Bull,
the evil outlaw,
will attack today."

King Leo nodded.
"We must be ready,"
he said.

Castles

Castles were built
in the Middle Ages.
People and animals
were safe there,
if an enemy attacked.

It was almost time for the feast.
Knights put on their armour.
Children washed at the well.

Armour
Knights wore armour made of
iron and steel for protection.
Special hinges let them move
their arms and legs!

Cedric the Bull watched
from the dark forest.
He could see everyone
getting ready.
"Not long now," he told his deputy,
Gilbert the Bad.

"Let the tournament begin!"
called King Leo.
Richard the Strong took part
in the first contest.
The horses galloped forwards.
The weapons clashed.
Sir Richard won.
"Well done!"
cheered the king.

Tournaments

In peacetime, knights trained by taking part in pretend battles, called tournaments. Some fought with long spears, called lances.

Cedric the Bull and Gilbert the Bad
hid behind the castle.

They had pushed an attack tower
up to the thick wall.

"Why did you make it so heavy?"
puffed Cedric.

"It has to carry twenty men,"
said Gilbert.

"We need it to climb the castle wall.
Then we can capture the castle!"

Attack!

Careful planning was
needed for a surprise
attack. Armies could
not move quickly
as the soldiers wore
heavy armour and used
huge weapons.

King Leo was cheering the knights
when he heard a bugle call
above the noise of the crowd.

"It's the signal," he told his family.

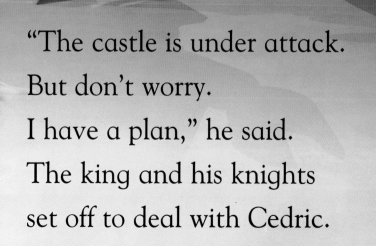

"The castle is under attack.
But don't worry.
I have a plan," he said.
The king and his knights
set off to deal with Cedric.

Cedric was a cowardly leader.
He did not really want to lead
his men up the tower.
"You must come, too,"
he told Gilbert.

The outlaws climbed the tower.
"Nearly there," panted Cedric.
He looked up.
"Oh no! Yuk!"
he cried.
Smelly food and
horse droppings
poured onto the
outlaws' heads.

On top of the castle,
King Leo smiled.
"What a good plan,"
he laughed.

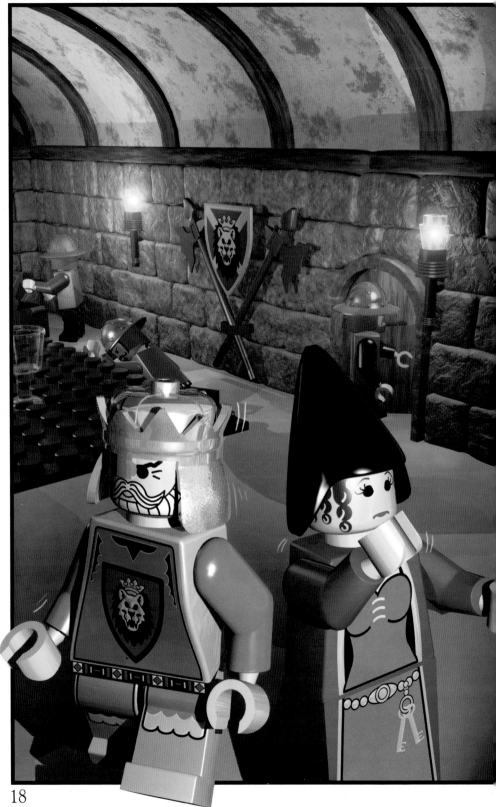

The king and his knights
went to the Great Hall.
The queen was waiting for them,
but Princess Storm was missing.
"Where's my daughter?"
the king asked.

A knight slipped away.
He was called
John of Mayne,
and the princess
was his friend.
He thought
he knew where
to find her.

Near the forest,
there was a garden.
It was where
the princess sat,
when she felt sad.

Storm was unhappy because
she wanted to be a knight,
and help her father King Leo.
But girls were not allowed
to be knights.

Women's lives
Women did not have
much power. But when
the men were away
fighting, the women did
their work!

John could see the princess
sitting in the garden.
Before he could call to her,
someone appeared from the trees.
It was Gilbert the Bad.
He pulled Storm into the forest.

Gilbert took the princess
to the outlaws' hidden camp,
where Cedric was waiting.

"I'm not afraid of you,"
said Storm, bravely.
"I don't care," replied Cedric.
"I want the king's money.
Your father will pay me a high price
for your safe return."

Forests
In the Middle Ages,
forests were much
bigger than they are
now. Wood from the
trees was used to build
carts, ships and homes.

A bugle call rang out in the forest.
It was a signal to Cedric.
"The king himself is looking
for you!" he told Storm.

"While the king searches the forest, my outlaws will attack his castle!" said Cedric.

He sat down with Gilbert to plan the attack.

An outlaw kept watch in the treetops.

"I can see the king!" he called. "He is lost in the forest. It will take him hours to find his way out!"

Coat of arms

Each knight had his own coat of arms on his shield. He could be recognised when wearing armour.

Cedric and Gilbert were plotting,
and they forgot to watch the princess.
Storm quietly escaped into the trees.

"She doesn't matter," said Cedric.
"Why ask for a little bit of treasure?
Now we can take it all!"

Soon, Cedric and the outlaws
surrounded the castle.
They loaded a catapult
with a rock.
"Fire!"
said Cedric.

Weapons of war

Swords and lances were no use for attacking a castle. Instead, huge catapults hurled enormous rocks and did serious damage.

Then there came a shout.
The king rode out from the forest.
"You are surrounded!" he cried.
"Give up your weapons."
"We thought you were lost!"
said Cedric.

"It was a clever trick.
Sir Richard is wearing my armour!"
laughed the king.
"Now you are trapped!"

"I still have your daughter!"
Cedric lied to the king.
"Oh no, you don't!" called Storm,
running out from the trees.
"Hooray!" cheered the knights.
The outlaws were taken away.

That night, in the dungeons,
the outlaws could hear the feast.
Everyone was very happy,
apart from the outlaws, of course.

"I'm not finished yet,"
Cedric said, in a horrible whisper.
"Just you wait, King Leo!
Just you wait!"

Knights and castles facts

A knight was a soldier,
who rode a horse in battle.
He fought for a lord
or king.

Feasts were held in
the Great Hall.
They started early.
People began eating by
11 o'clock in the morning.
The meal lasted for hours.

A suit of armour cost
about £50,000, in today's
money. That is more than
most sports cars!

Only boys from rich
families were allowed to
train as knights.

A boy started training
to be a knight
at the age of seven.

It could take a knight
up to one hour
to put on all his armour.

Most castles were built
in a time called
the Middle Ages.
This lasted from around
AD 450 to 1500.

The first castles
were built from wood.
It was easy to
burn them down.
So then, builders started
to use stone.

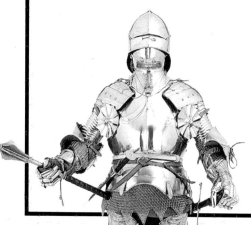